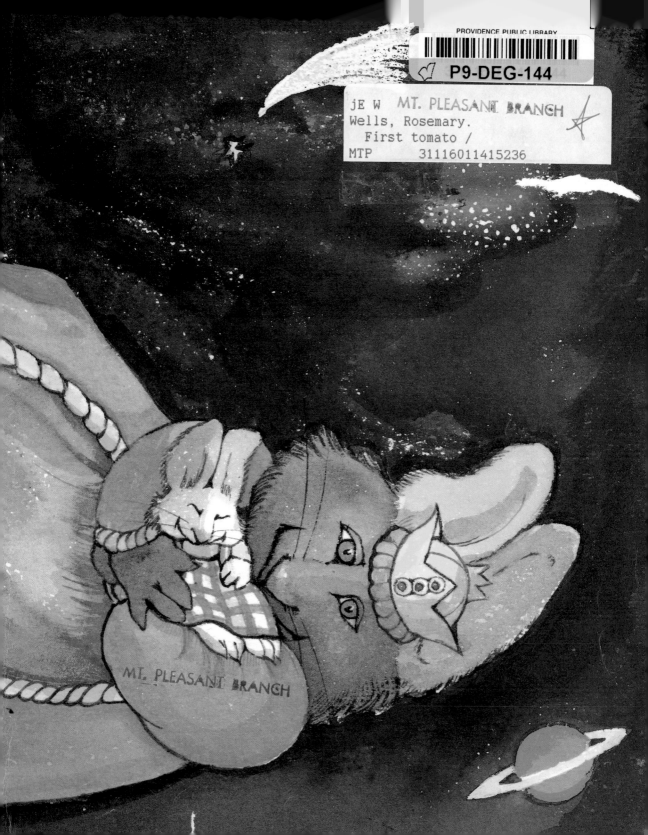

PROVIDENCE PUBLIC LIBRARY

P9-DEG-144

jE W   MT. PLEASANT BRANCH
Wells, Rosemary.
   First tomato /
MTP   31116011415236

MT. PLEASANT BRANCH

· A VOYAGE TO THE BUNNY PLANET ·

FIRST TOMATO

Rosemary Wells

DIAL BOOKS FOR YOUNG READERS
NEW YORK

Published by Dial Books for Young Readers
A Division of Penguin Books USA Inc.
375 Hudson Street · New York, New York 10014

Copyright © 1992 by Rosemary Wells
All rights reserved
Printed in the U.S.A.
Design by Atha Tehon
First Edition
1 3 5 7 9 10 8 6 4 2

Library of Congress Cataloging in Publication Data
Wells, Rosemary.
First tomato / Rosemary Wells.—1st ed.
p.   cm.— (Voyage to the Bunny Planet)
Summary: Claire's bad day at school is helped after a visit to the Bunny Planet,
where she has the day that should have been.
ISBN 0-8037-1175-1 (lib. bdg.)
[1. Rabbits—Fiction. 2. Schools—Fiction.]   I. Title.
II. Series: Wells, Rosemary. Voyage to the Bunny Planet.
PZ7.W46843Fl   1992   [E]—dc20   91-41599   CIP   AC

THE BUNNY PLANET IN HISTORY

*It is the first duty of a flagging spirit to seek renewal
in the latitudes of whimsy. I, for one, dream on
beyond the five planets to a world without wickedness;
verdant, mild, and populated by amiable lapins.*

Benjamin Franklin (Letters to a nephew, 1771)

Claire ate only three spoons
of cornflakes for breakfast.

On the way to school
her shoes filled with snow.

By eleven in the morning,
math had been going on for two hours.

Lunch was Claire's least favorite—
baloney sandwiches.

At playtime Claire was the only girl
not able to do a cartwheel.
Once again the bus was late.

Claire needs a visit to the Bunny Planet.

Far beyond the moon and stars,
Twenty light-years south of Mars,

Spins the gentle Bunny Planet
And the Bunny Queen is Janet.

Janet says to Claire, "Come in.

Here's the day that should have been."

I hear my mother calling when the summer wind blows,
   "Go out in the garden in your old, old clothes.

Pick me some runner beans and sugar snap peas.
Find a ripe tomato and bring it to me, please."

A ruby red tomato is hanging on the vine.

If my mother didn't want it, the tomato would be mine.

It smells of rain and steamy earth and hot June sun.
In the whole tomato garden it's the only ripe one.
I close my eyes and breathe in its fat, red smell.
I wish that I could eat it now and never, never tell.

But I save it for my mother without another look.

I wash the beans and shell the peas

and watch my mother cook.

I hear my mother calling when the summer winds blow,

"I've made you First Tomato soup because I love you so."

Claire's big warm bus comes at last.
Out her window Claire sees the Bunny Planet
near the evening star in the snowy sky.
"It was there all along!" says Claire.

The other two Voyages to the Bunny Planet are:

MOSS PILLOWS

THE ISLAND LIGHT

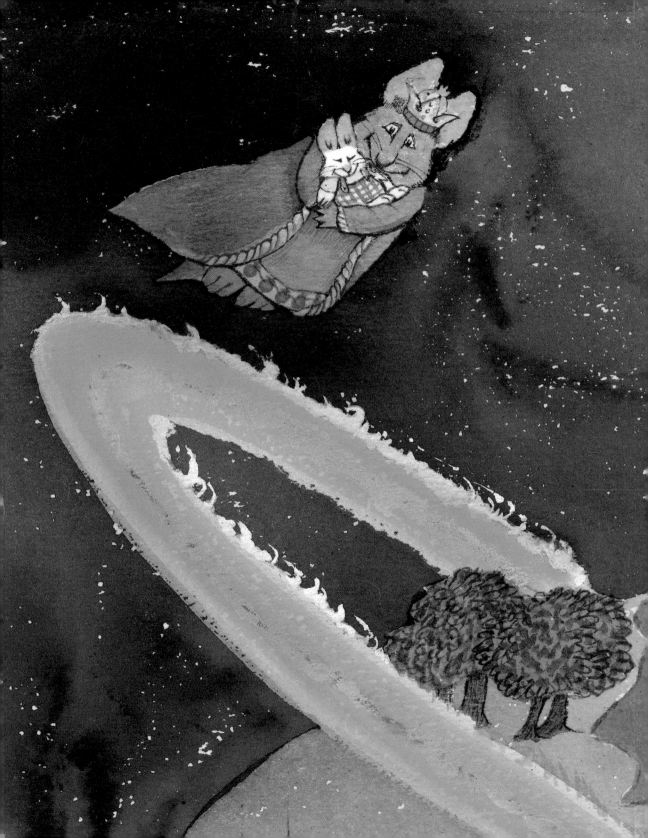